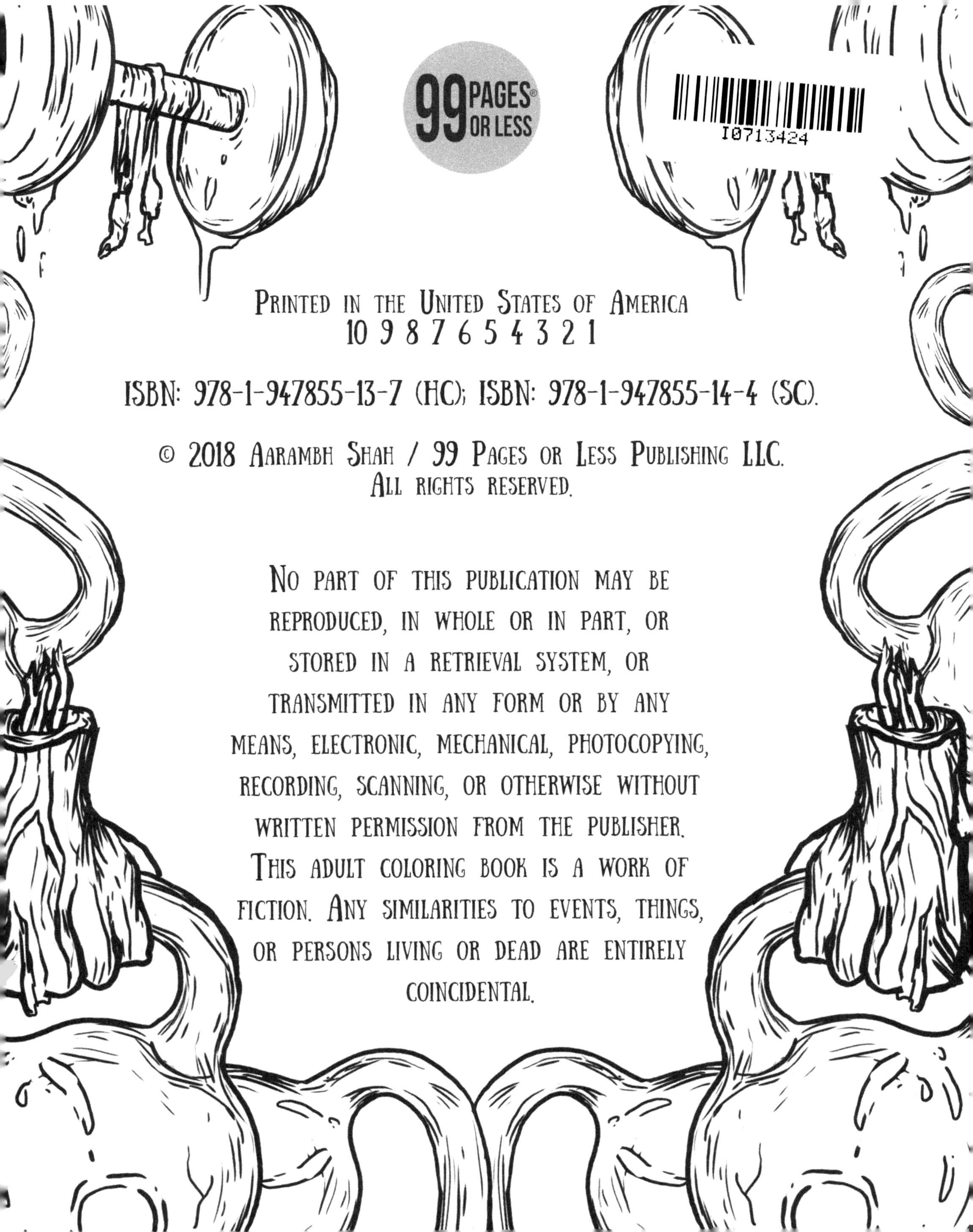

Printed in the United States of America
10 9 8 7 6 5 4 3 2 1

ISBN: 978-1-947855-13-7 (HC); ISBN: 978-1-947855-14-4 (SC).

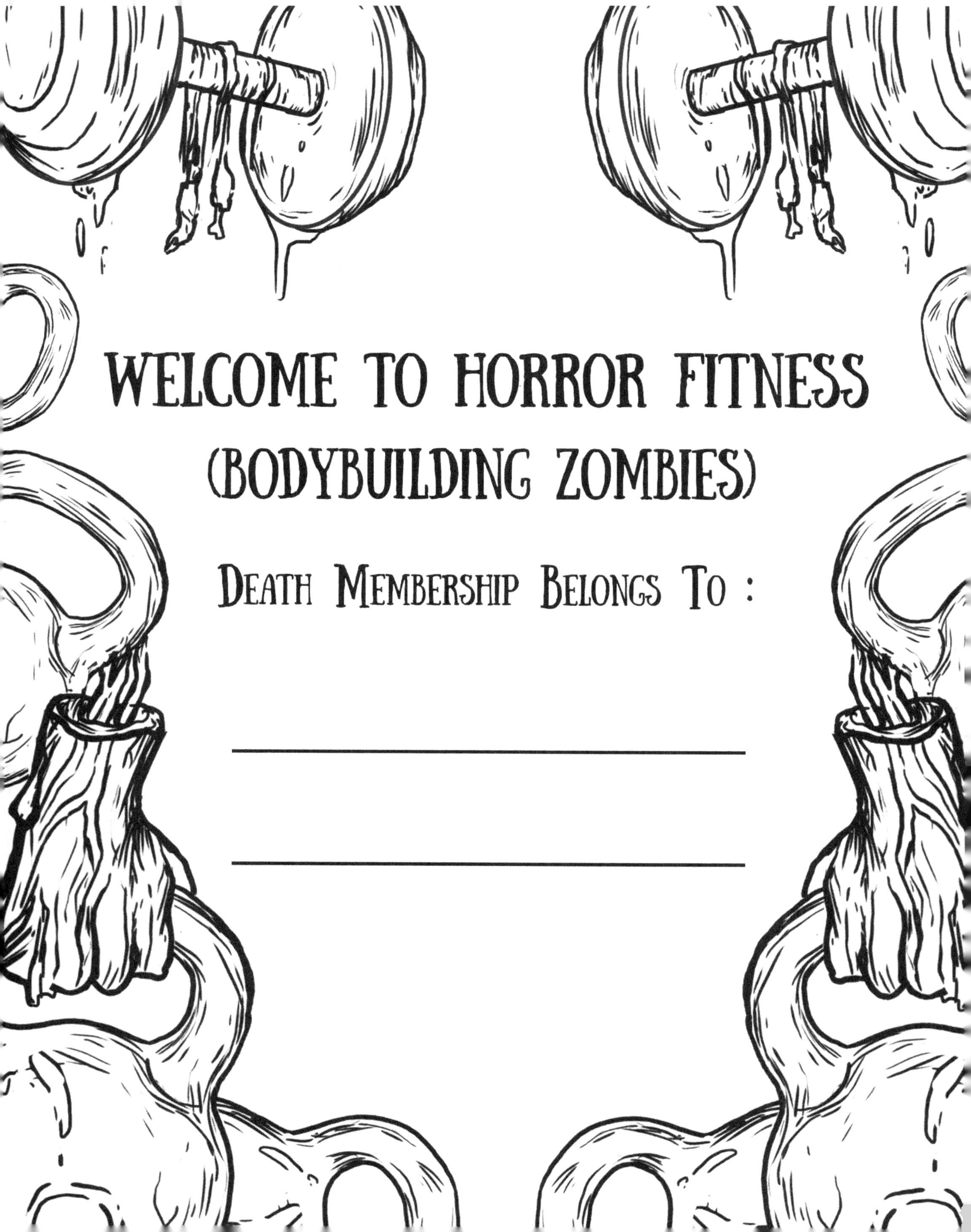

WELCOME TO HORROR FITNESS
(BODYBUILDING ZOMBIES)
DEATH MEMBERSHIP BELONGS TO :

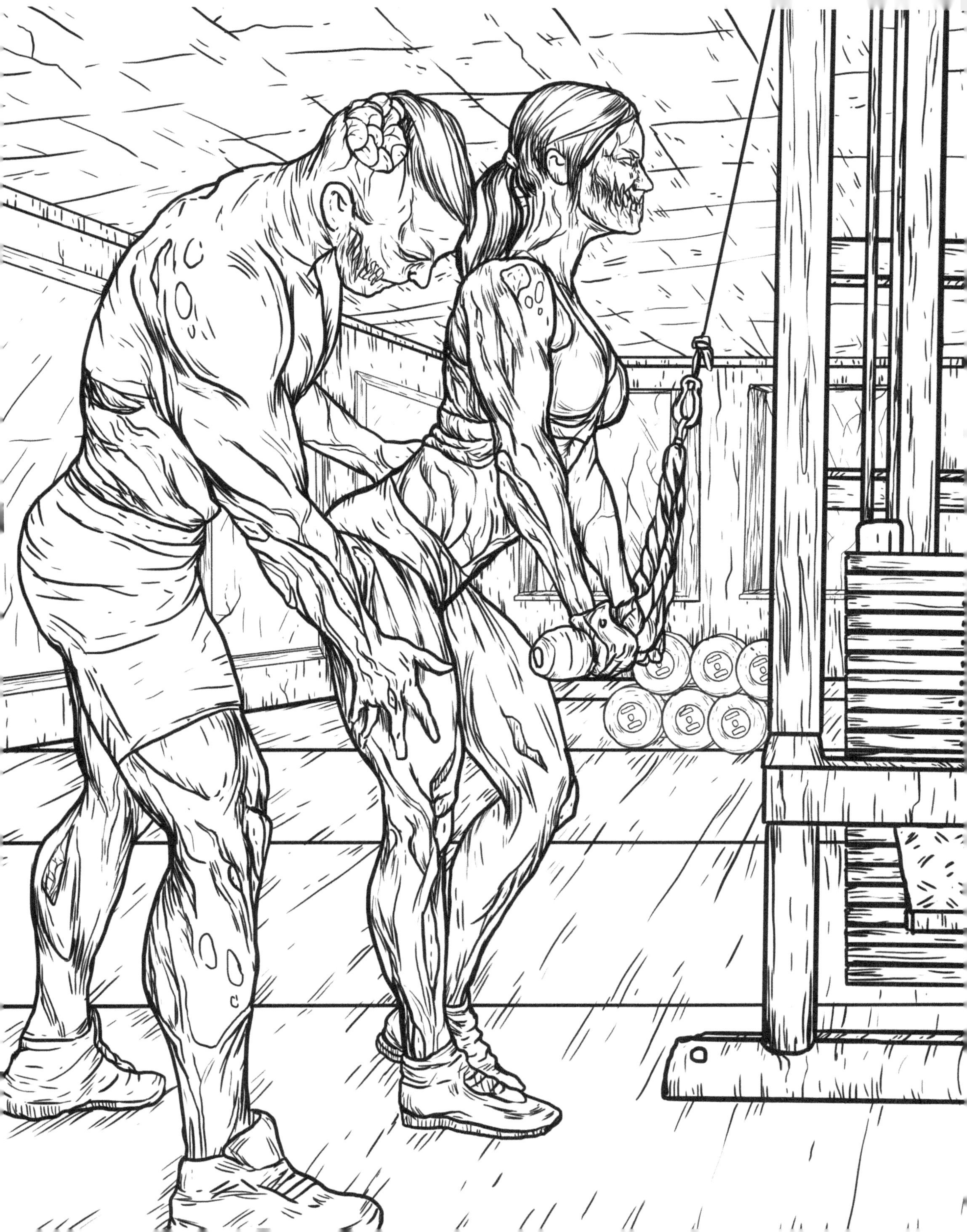

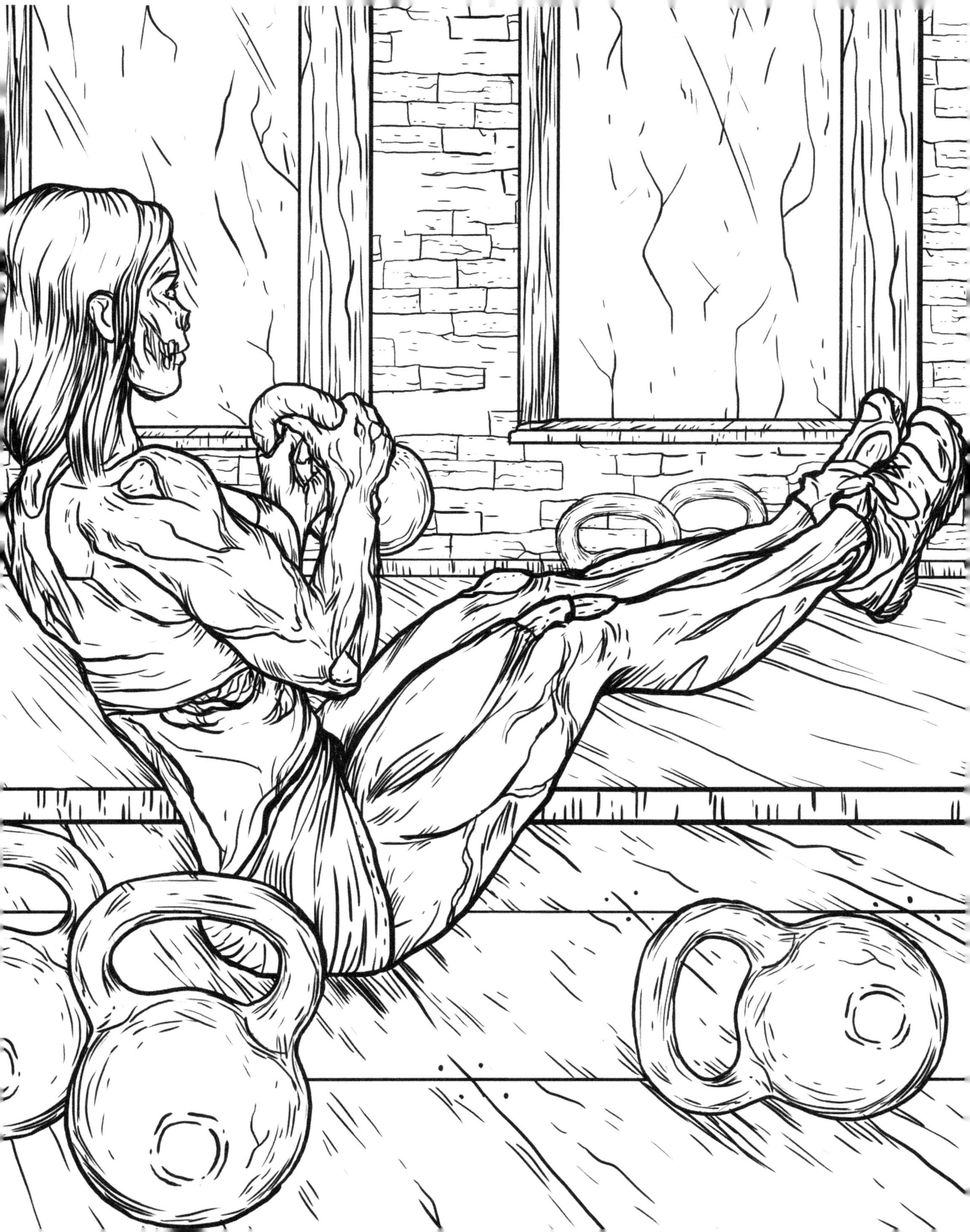

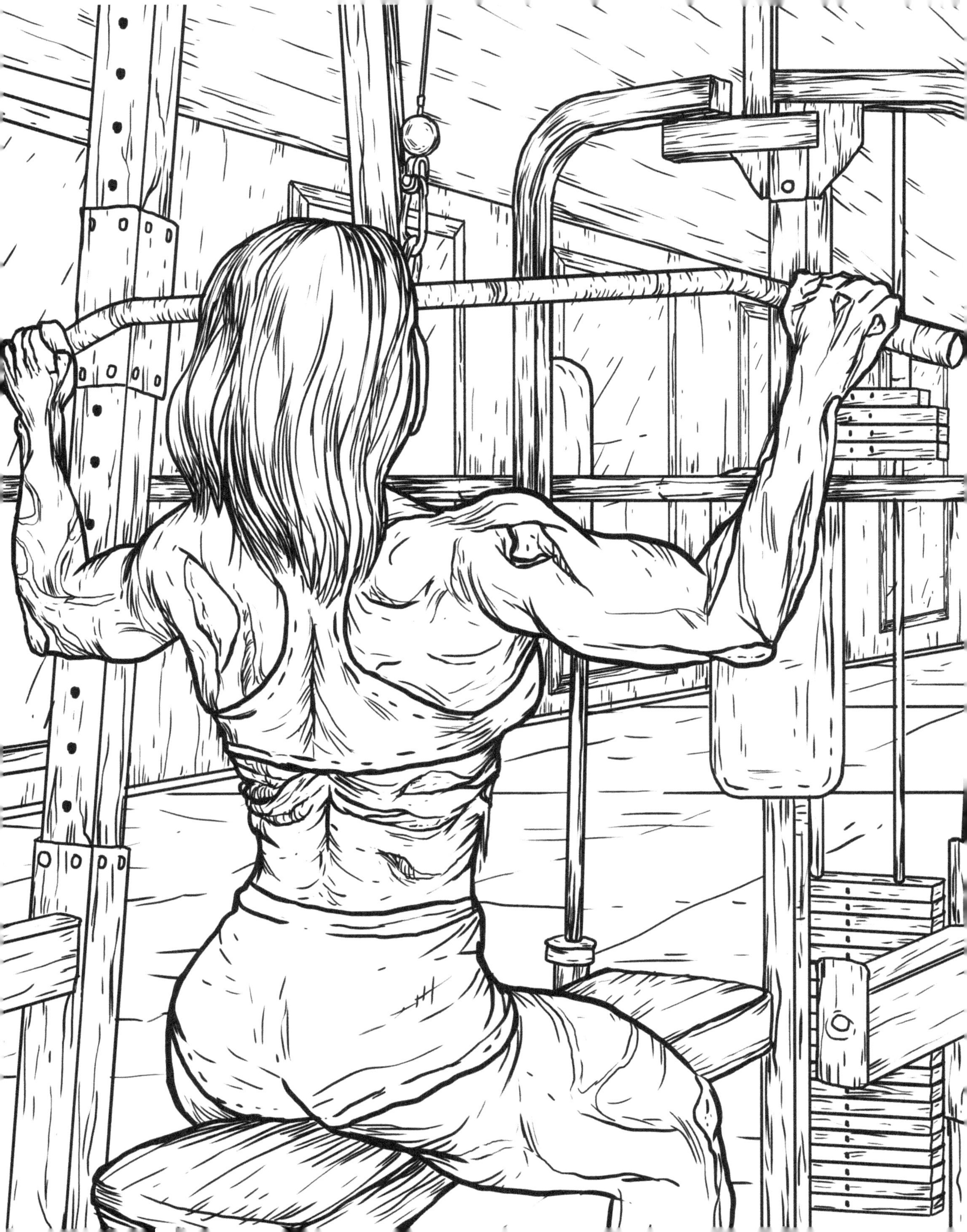

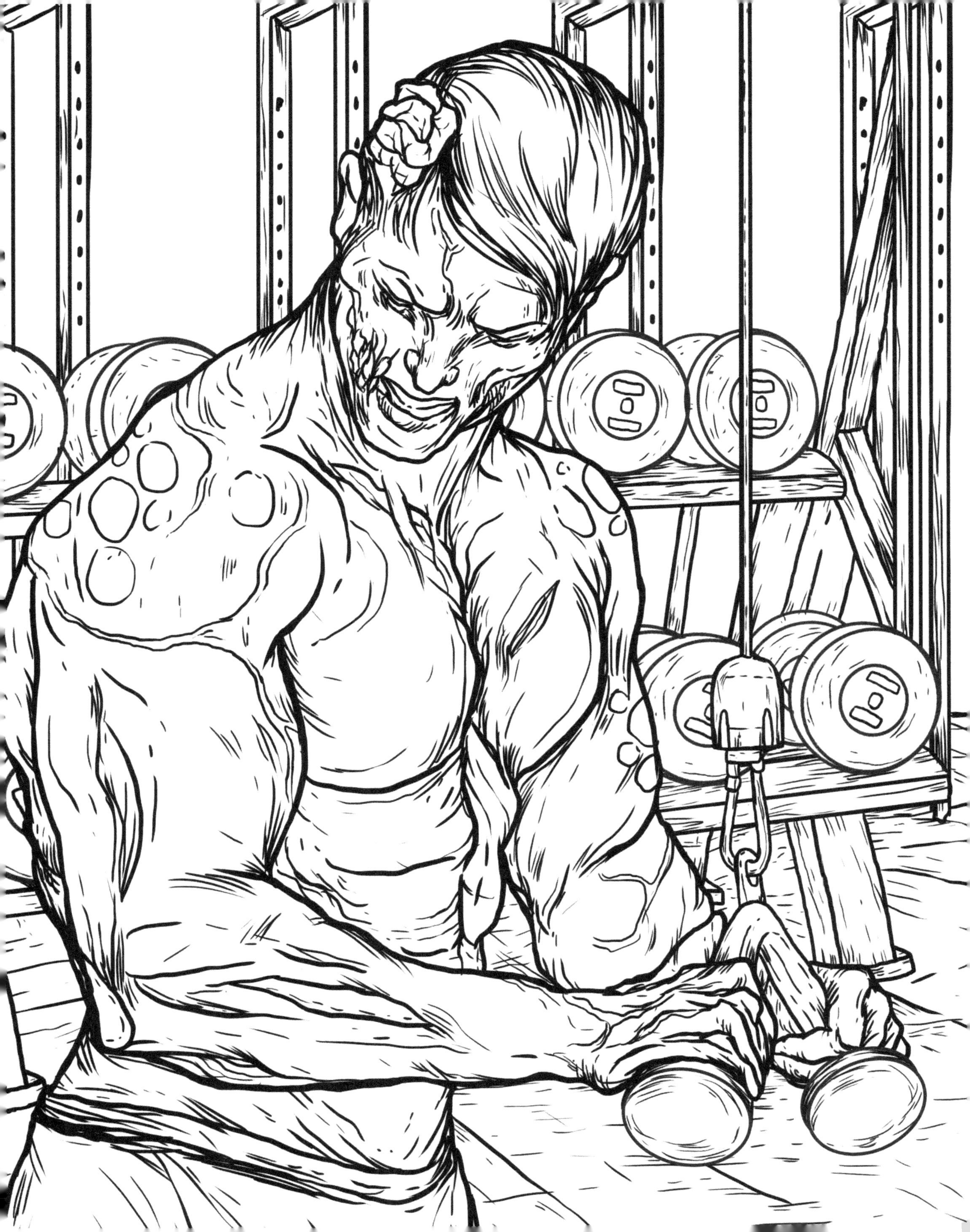

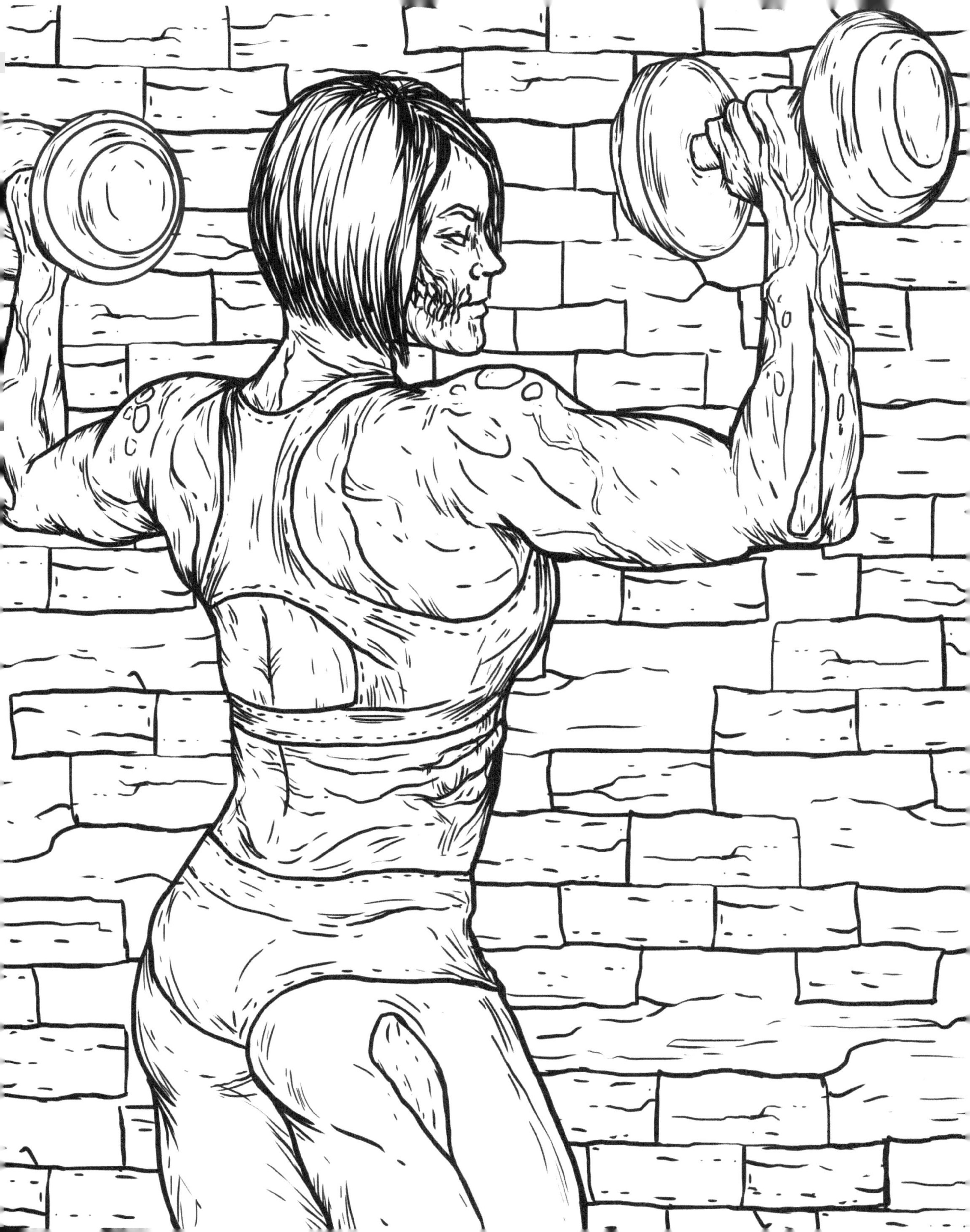

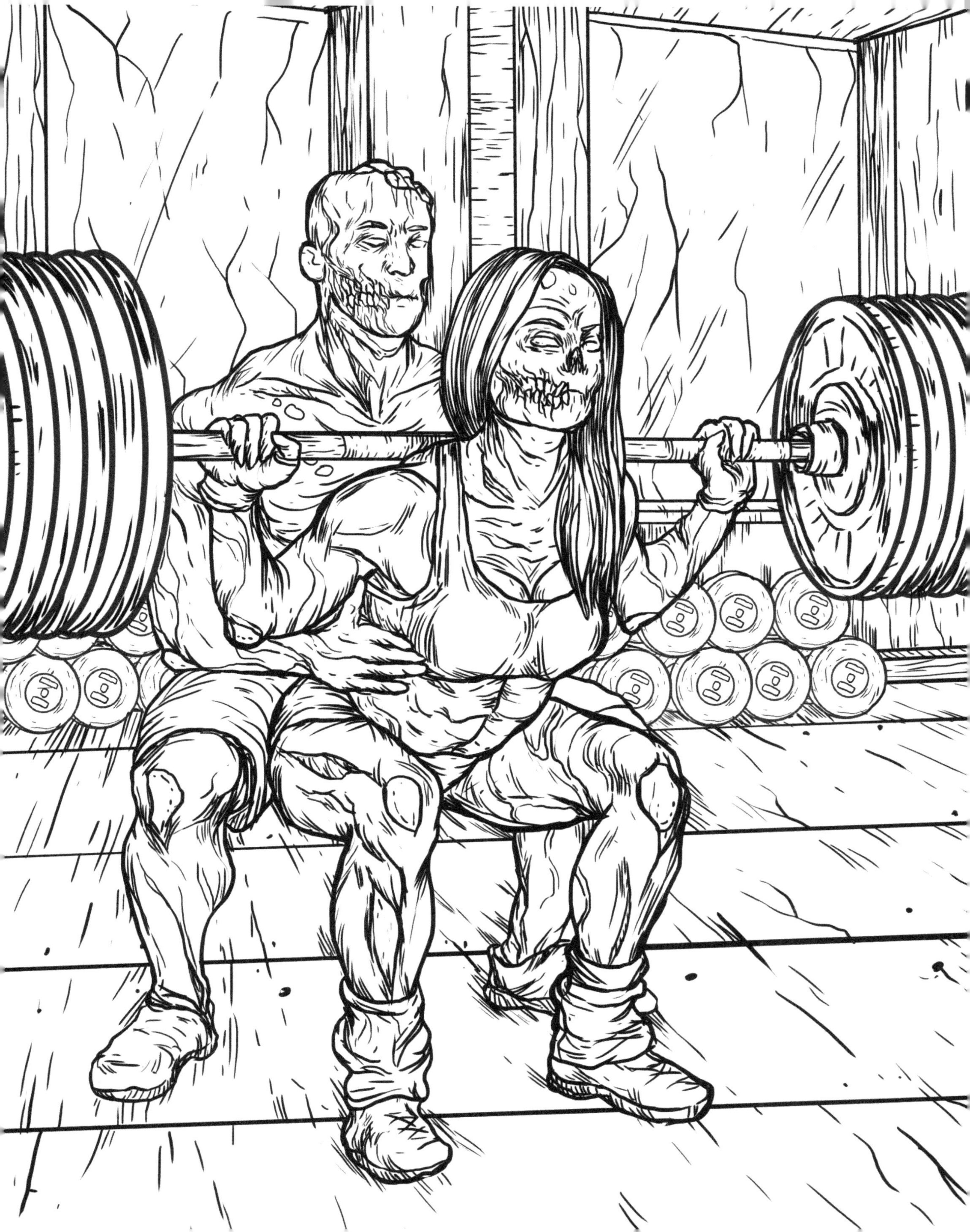

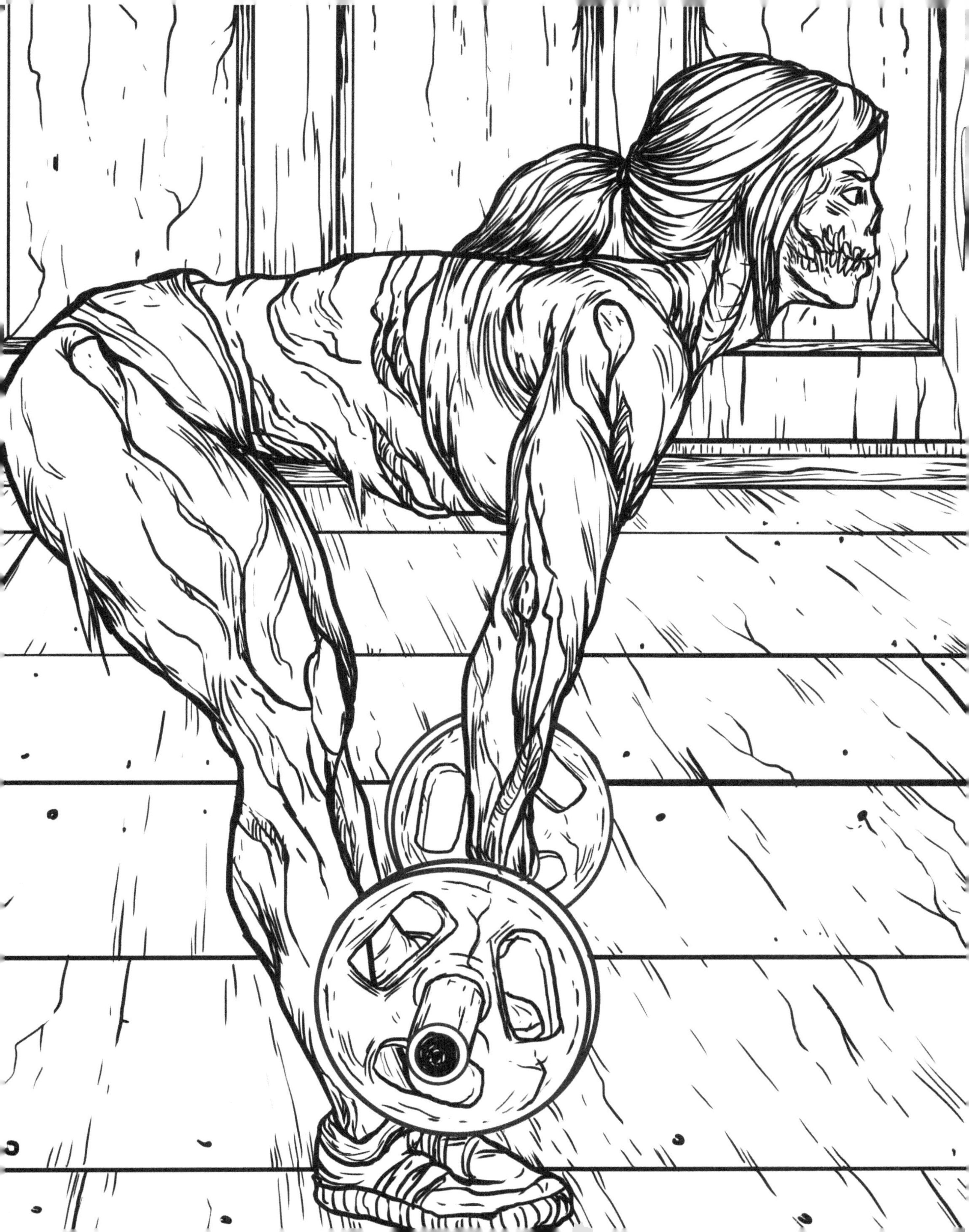

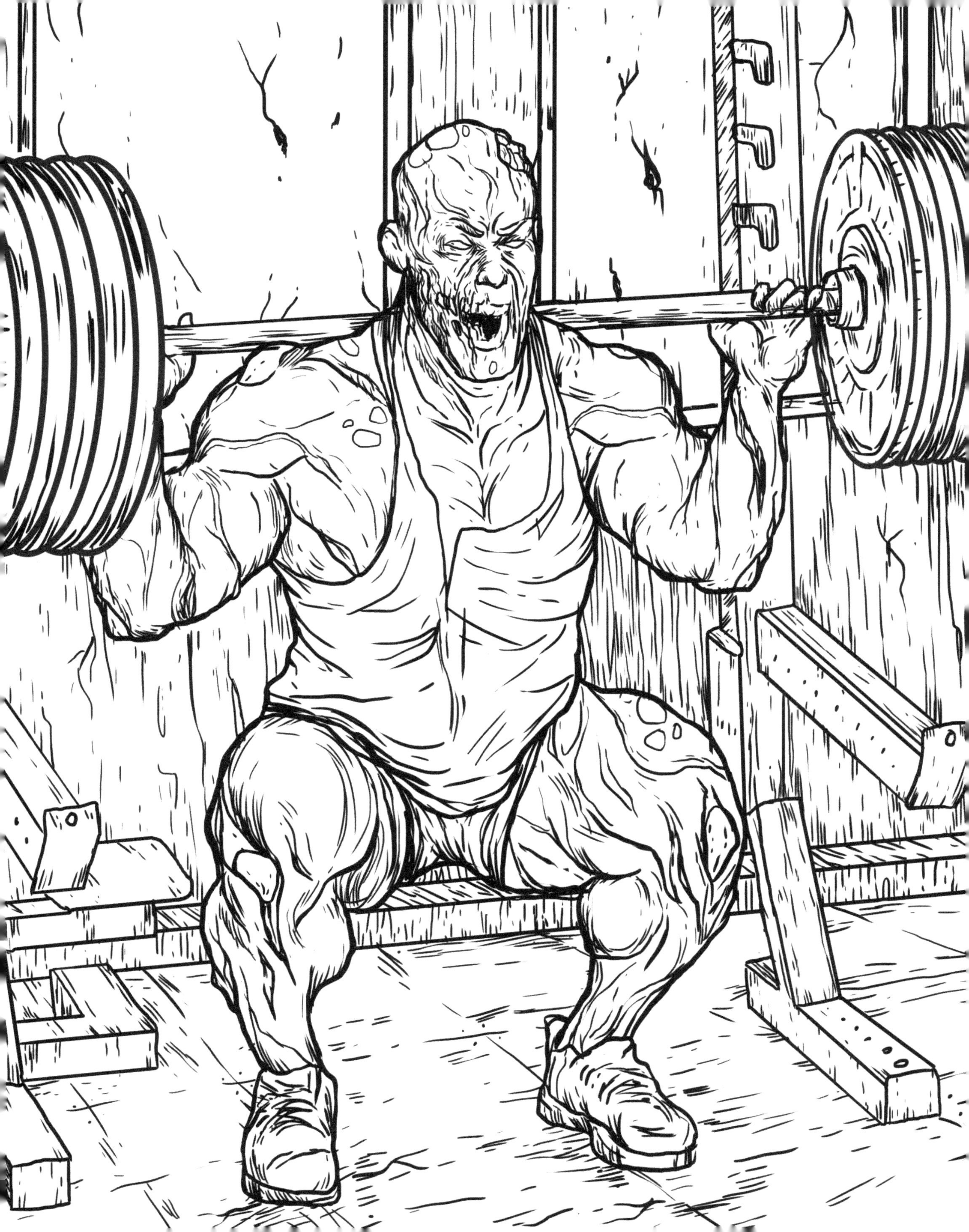

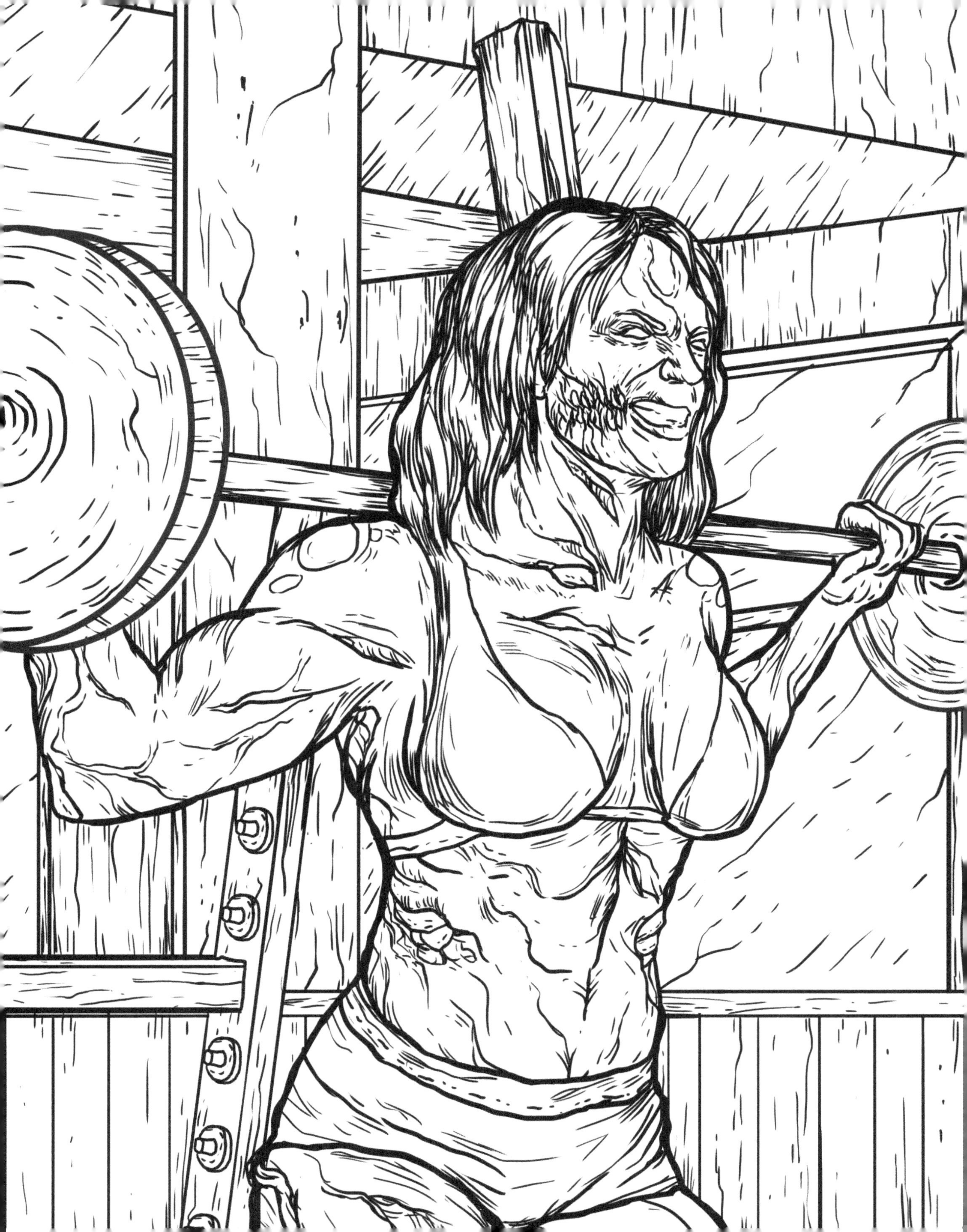

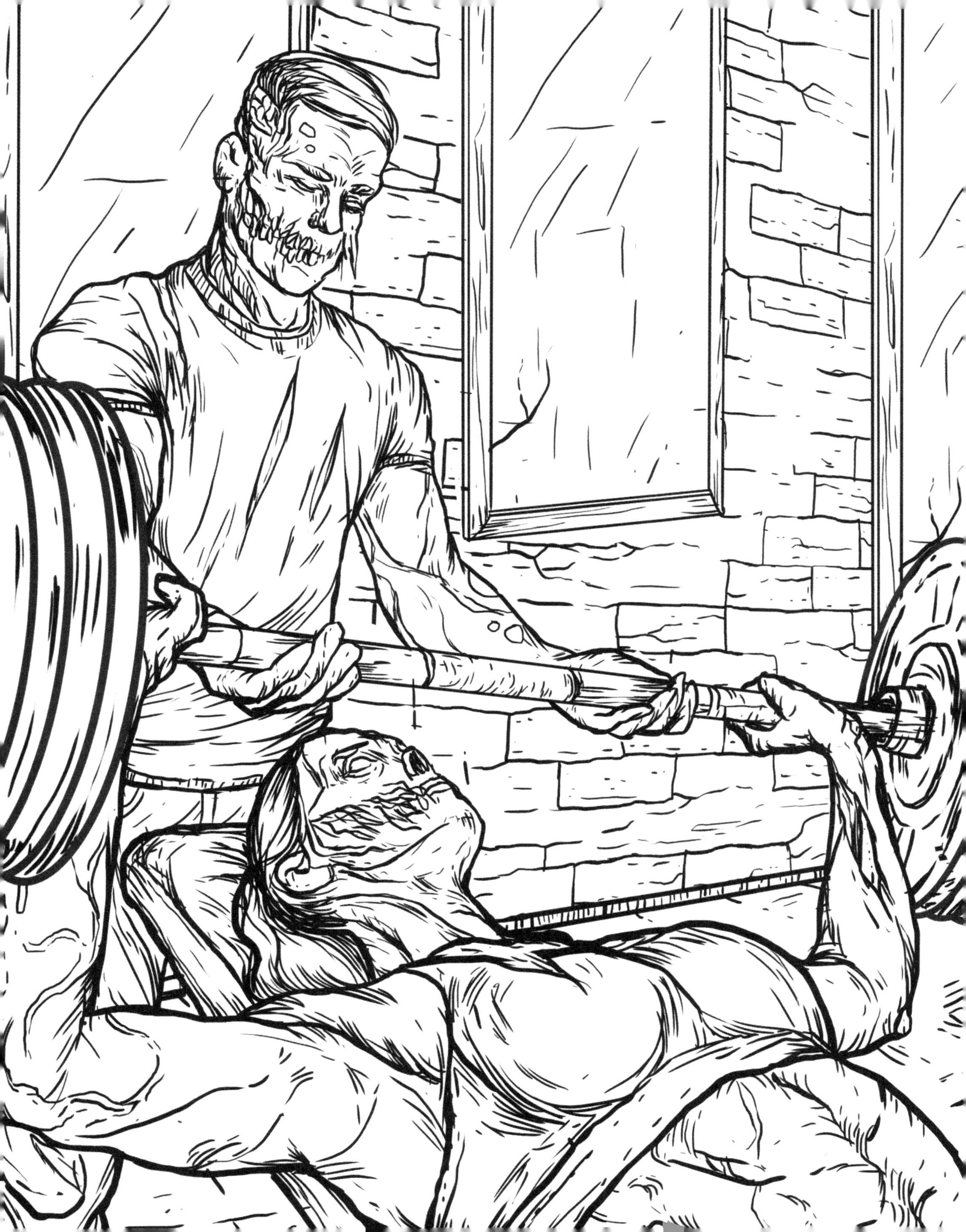

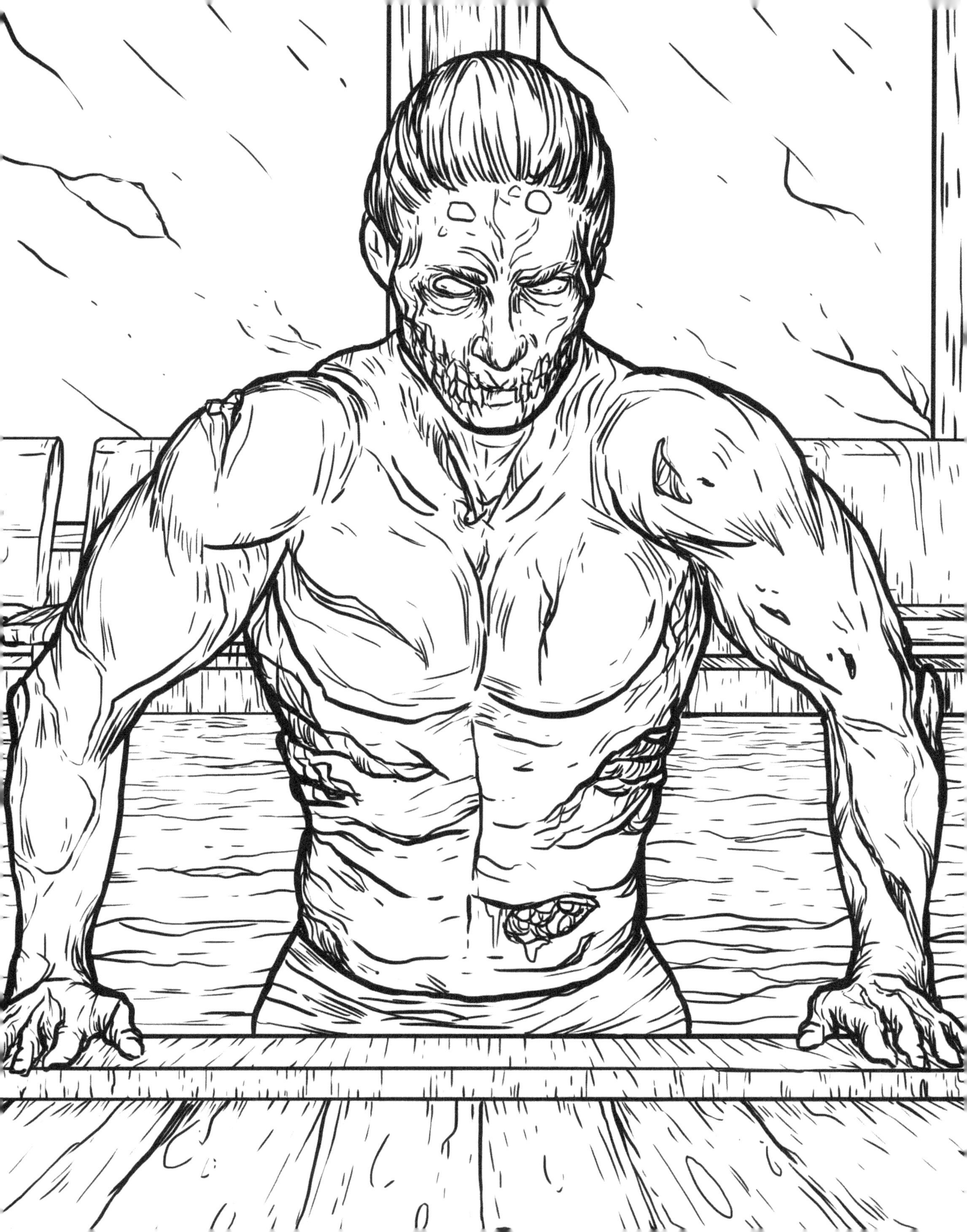

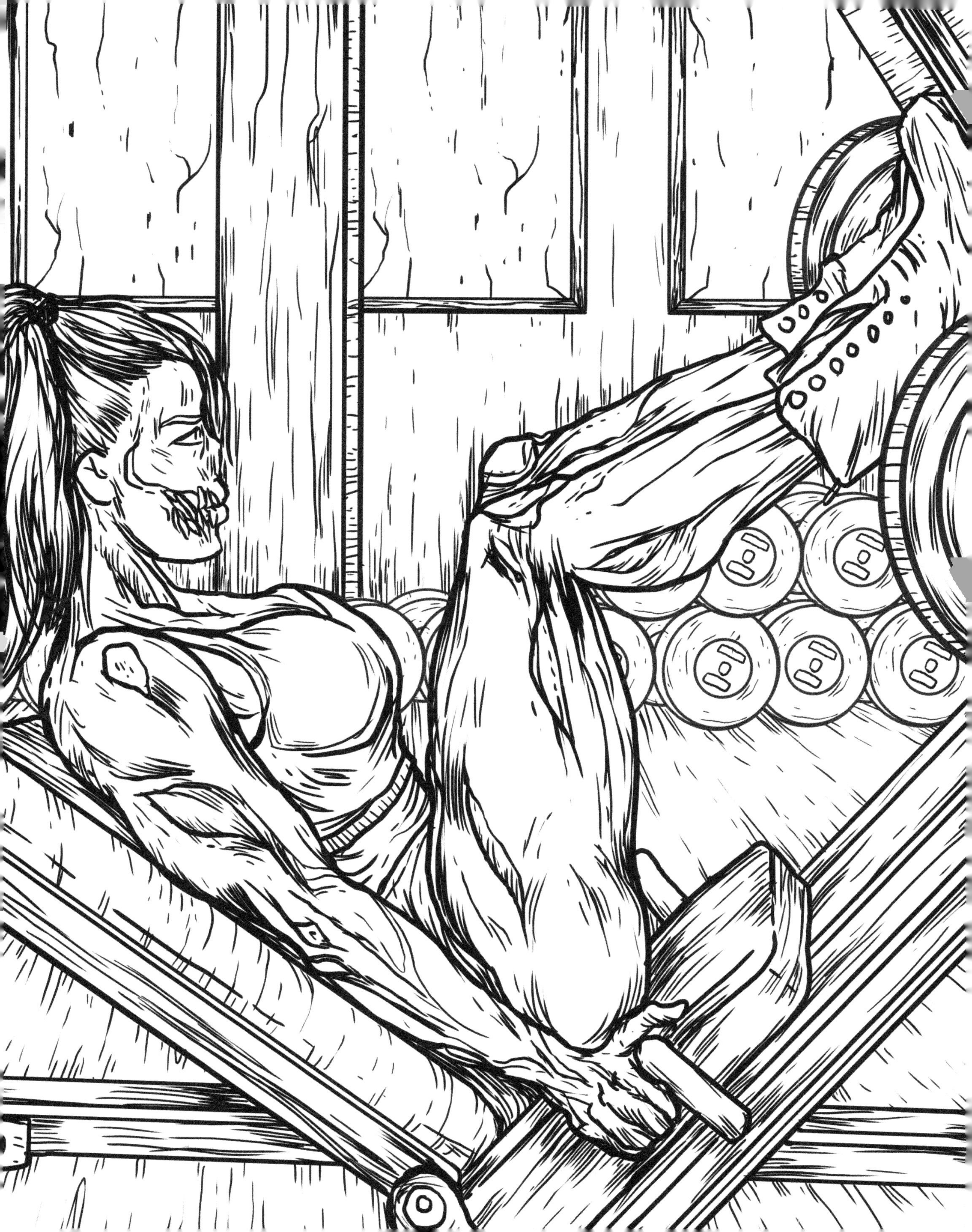

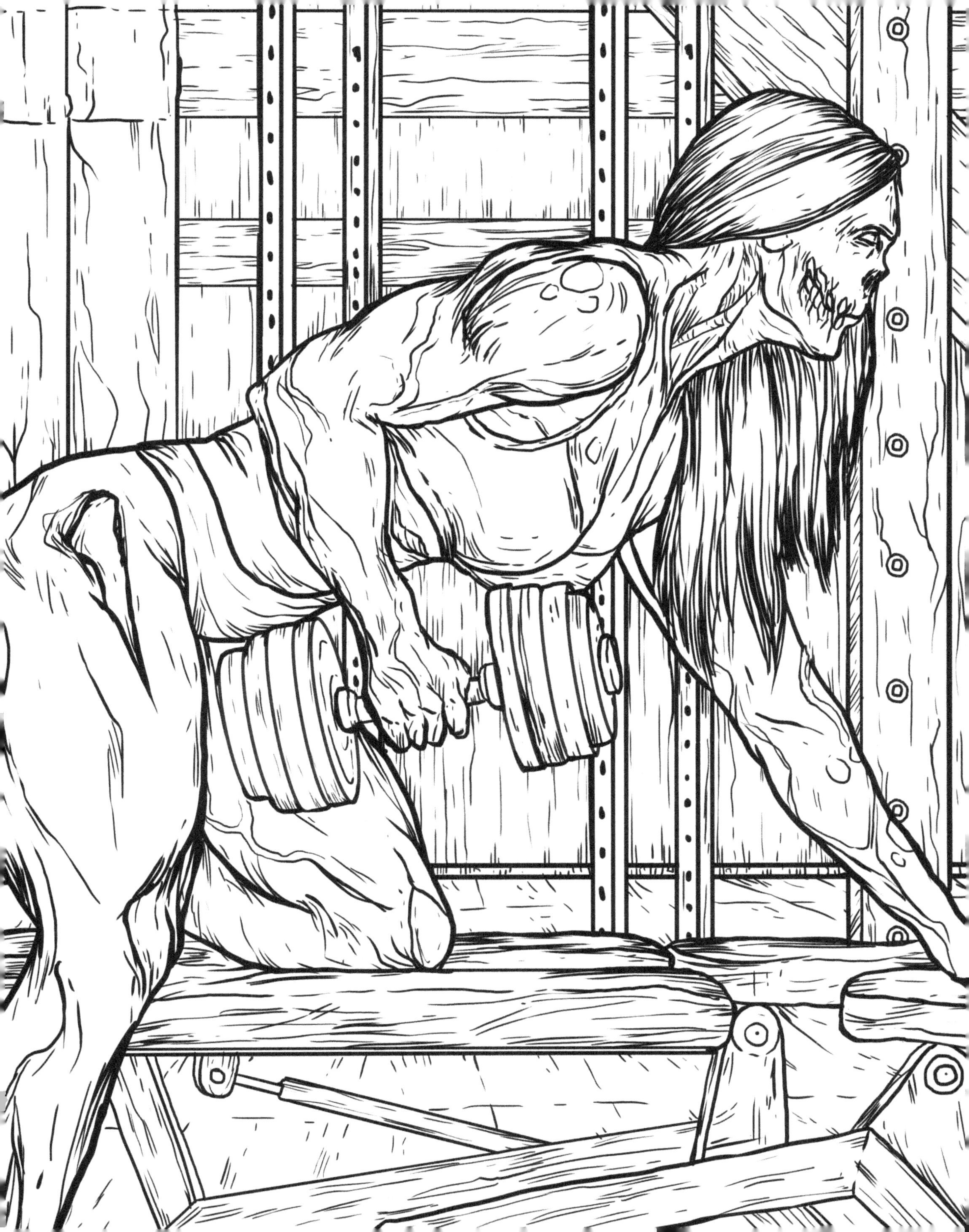

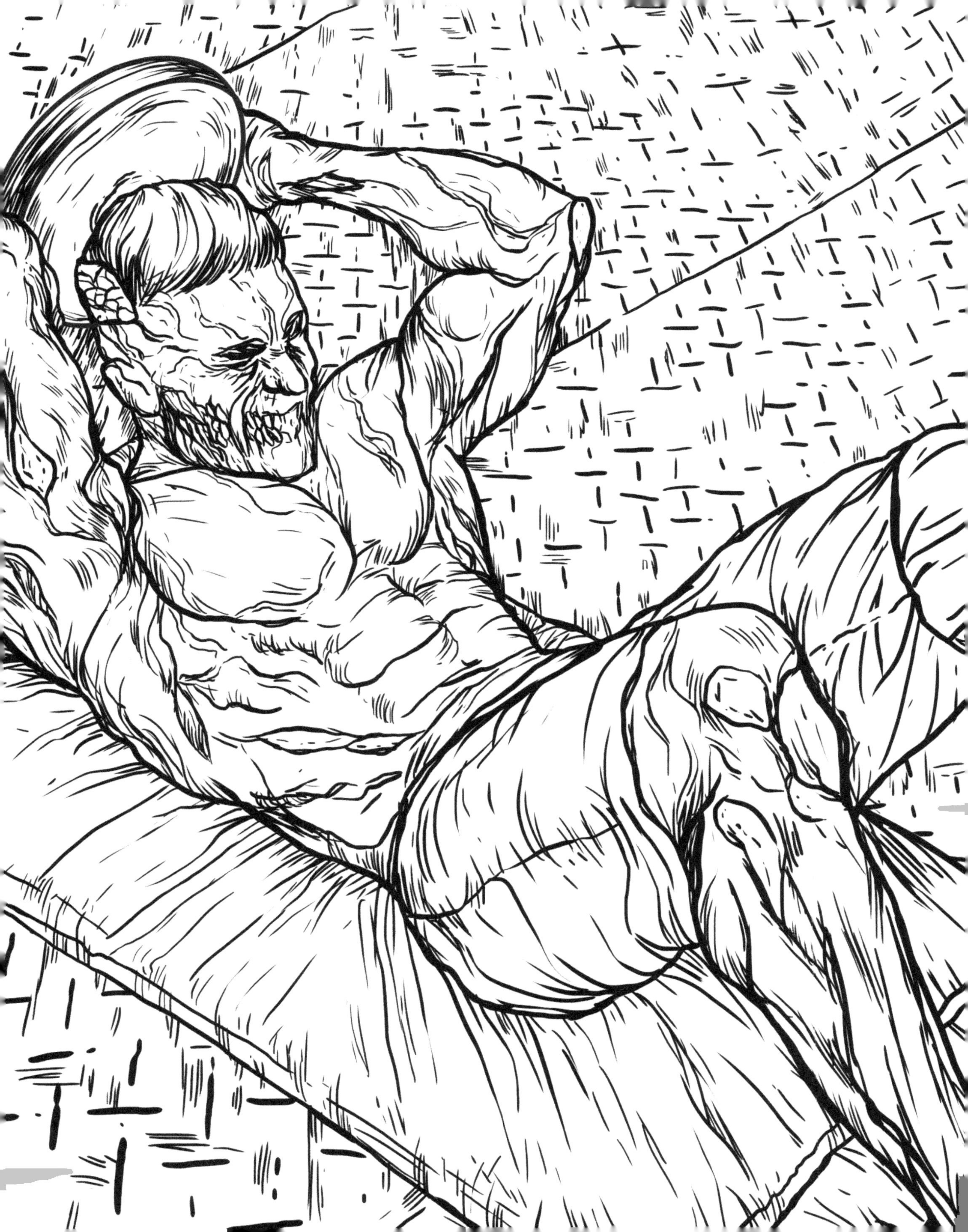

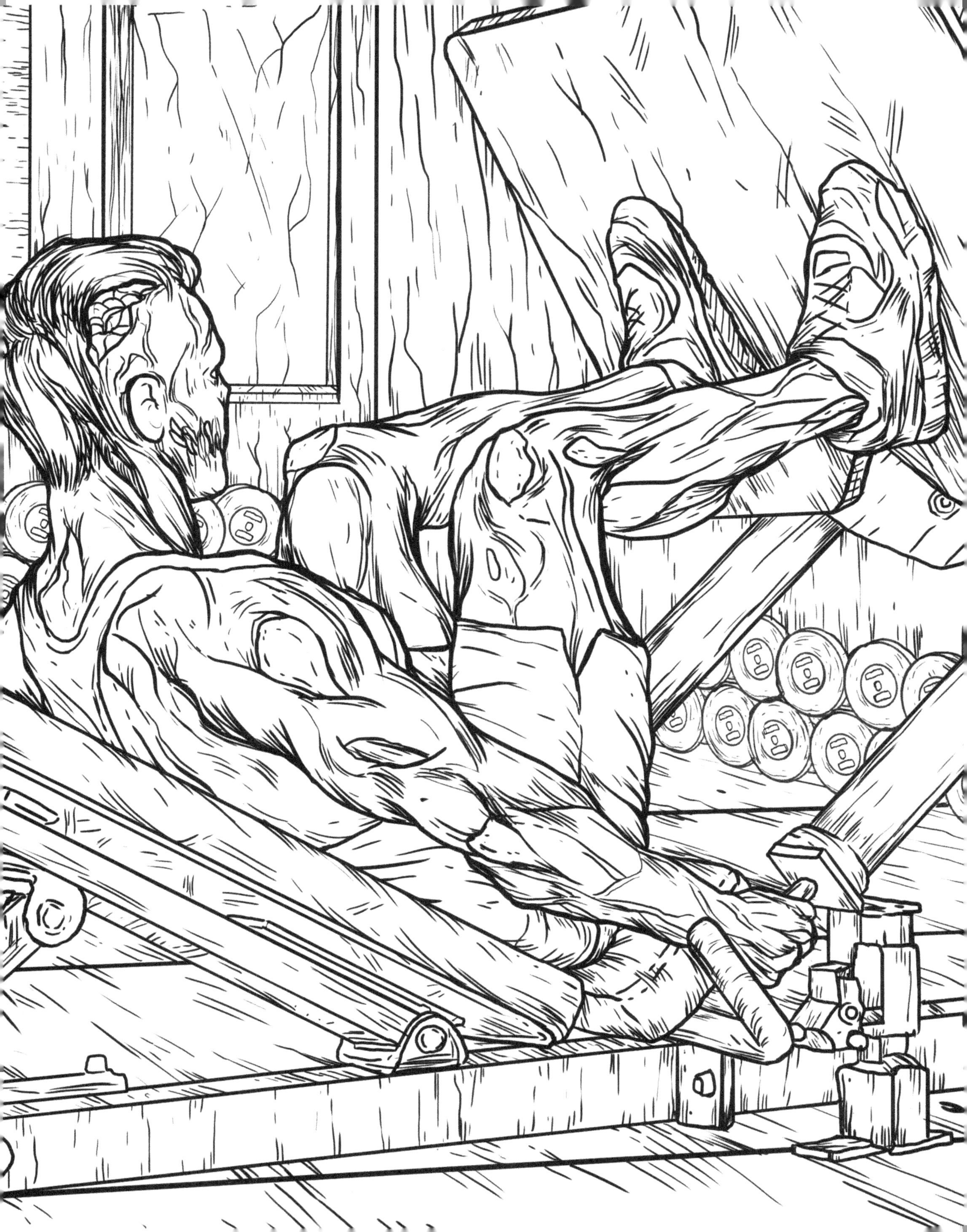

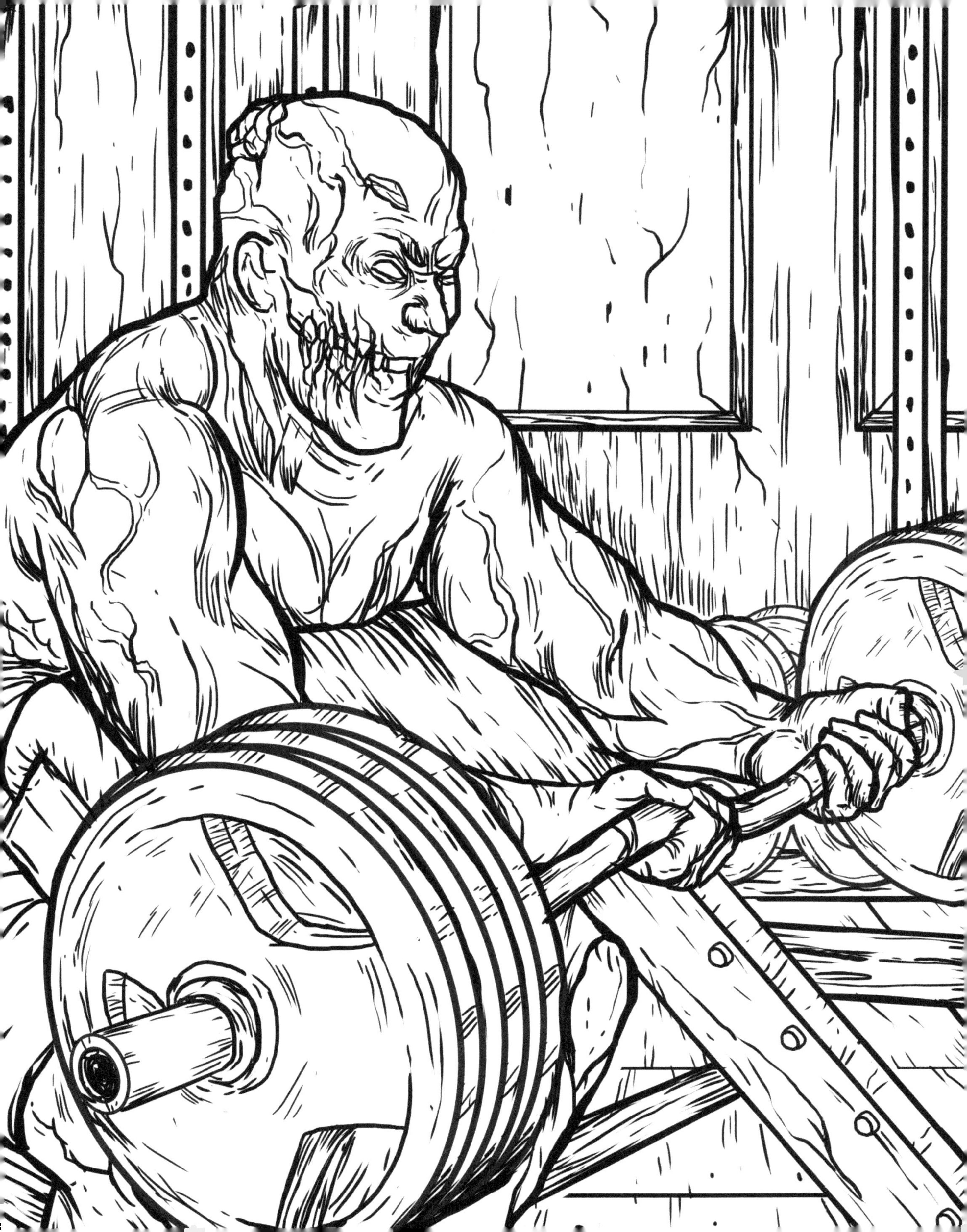

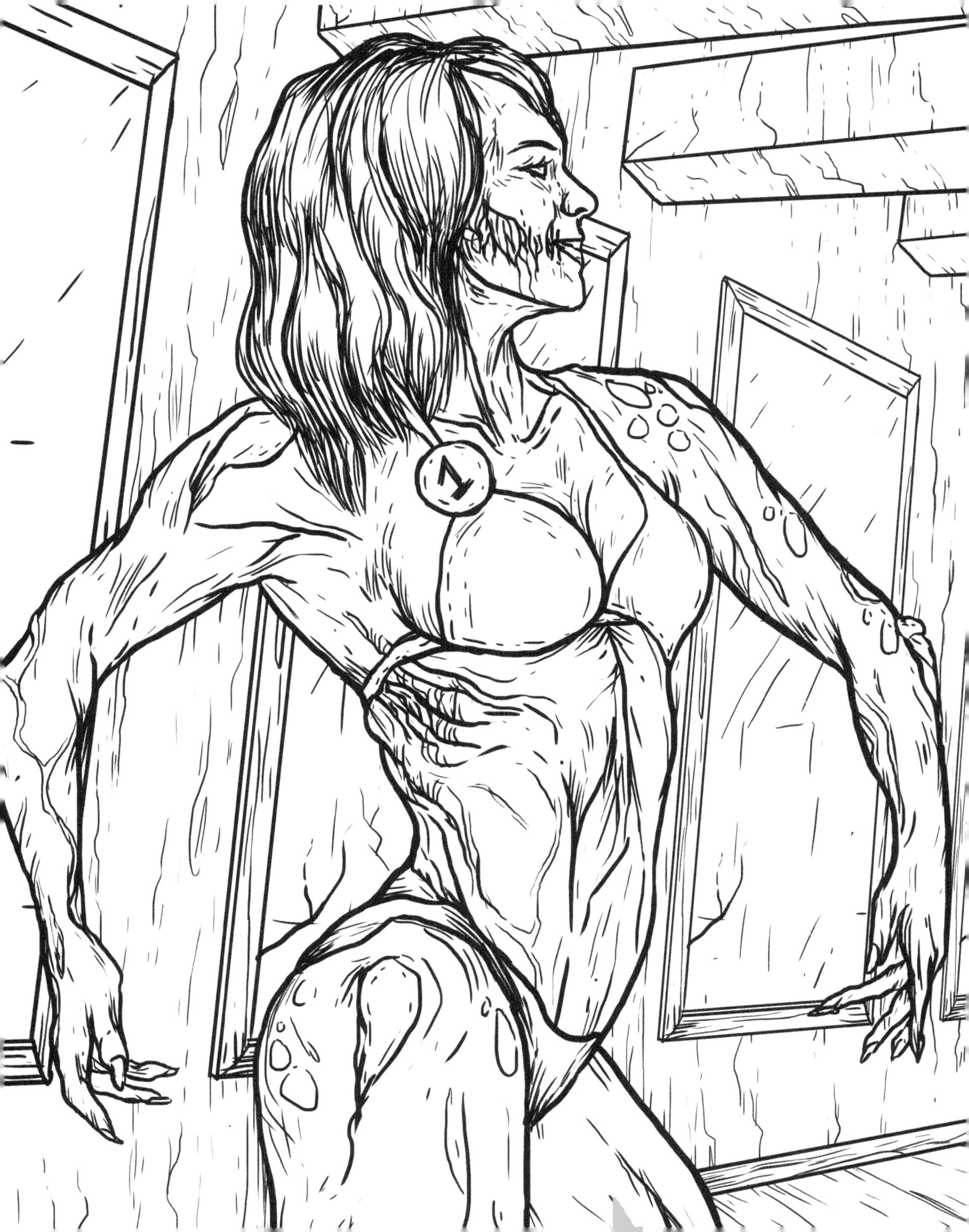

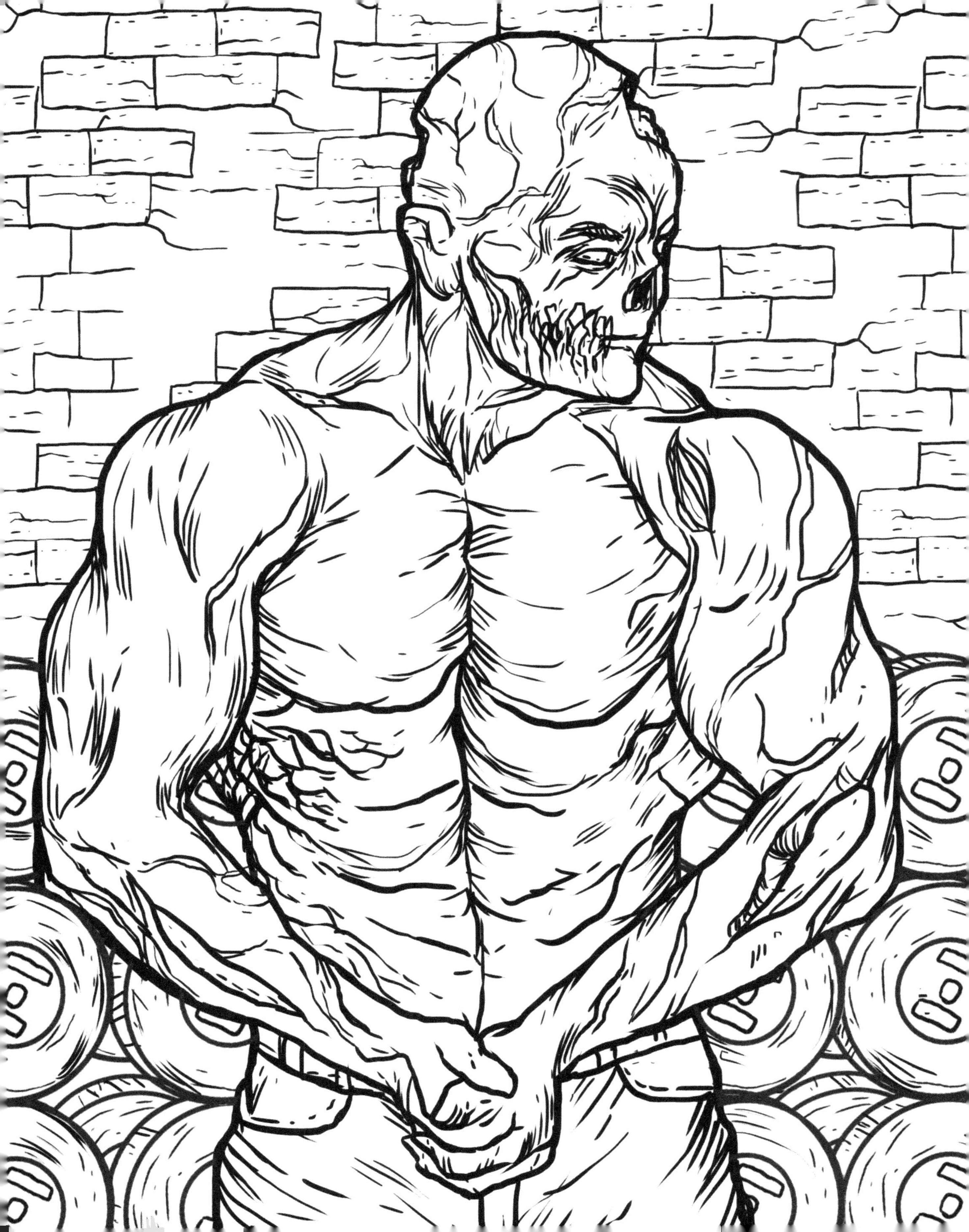

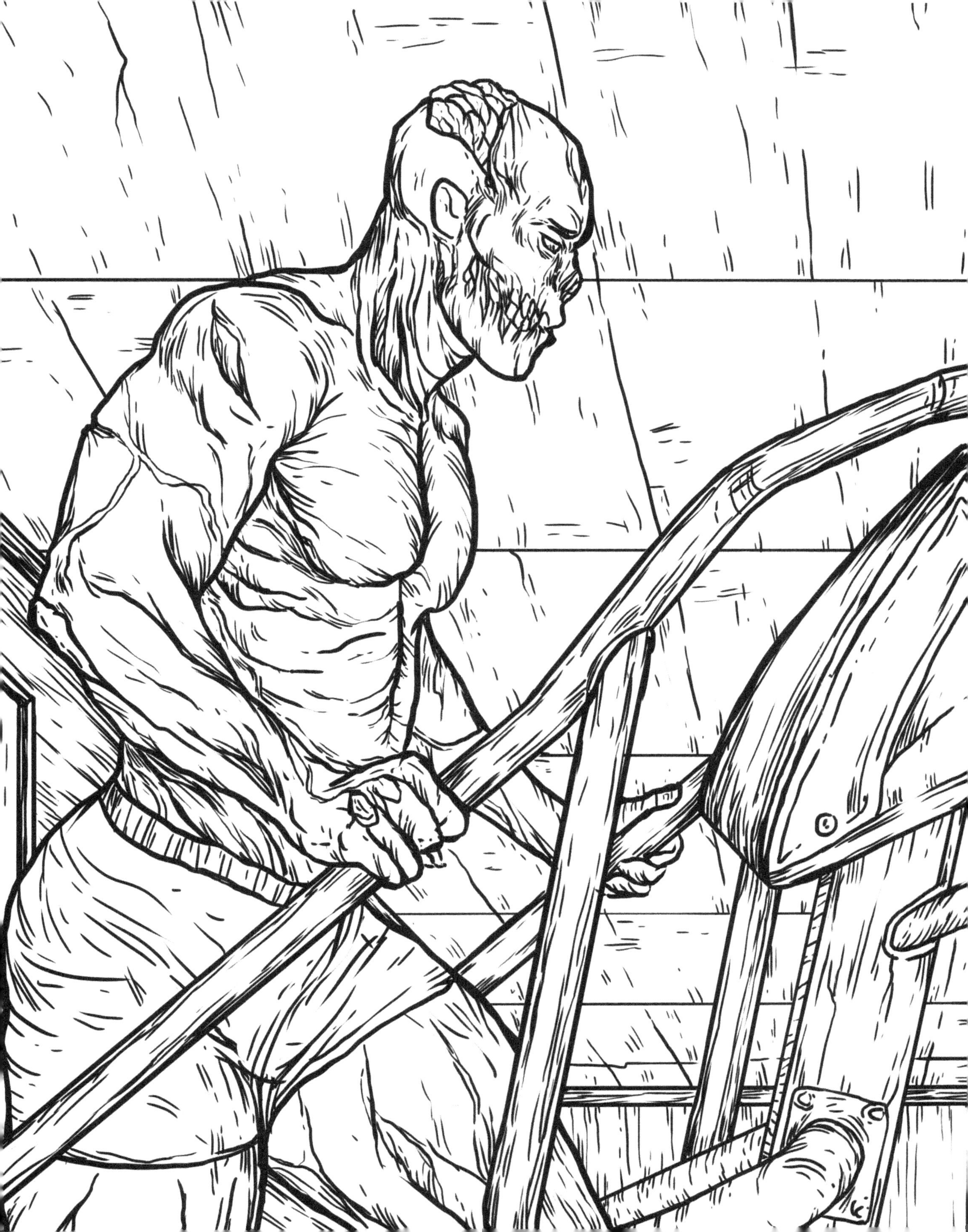

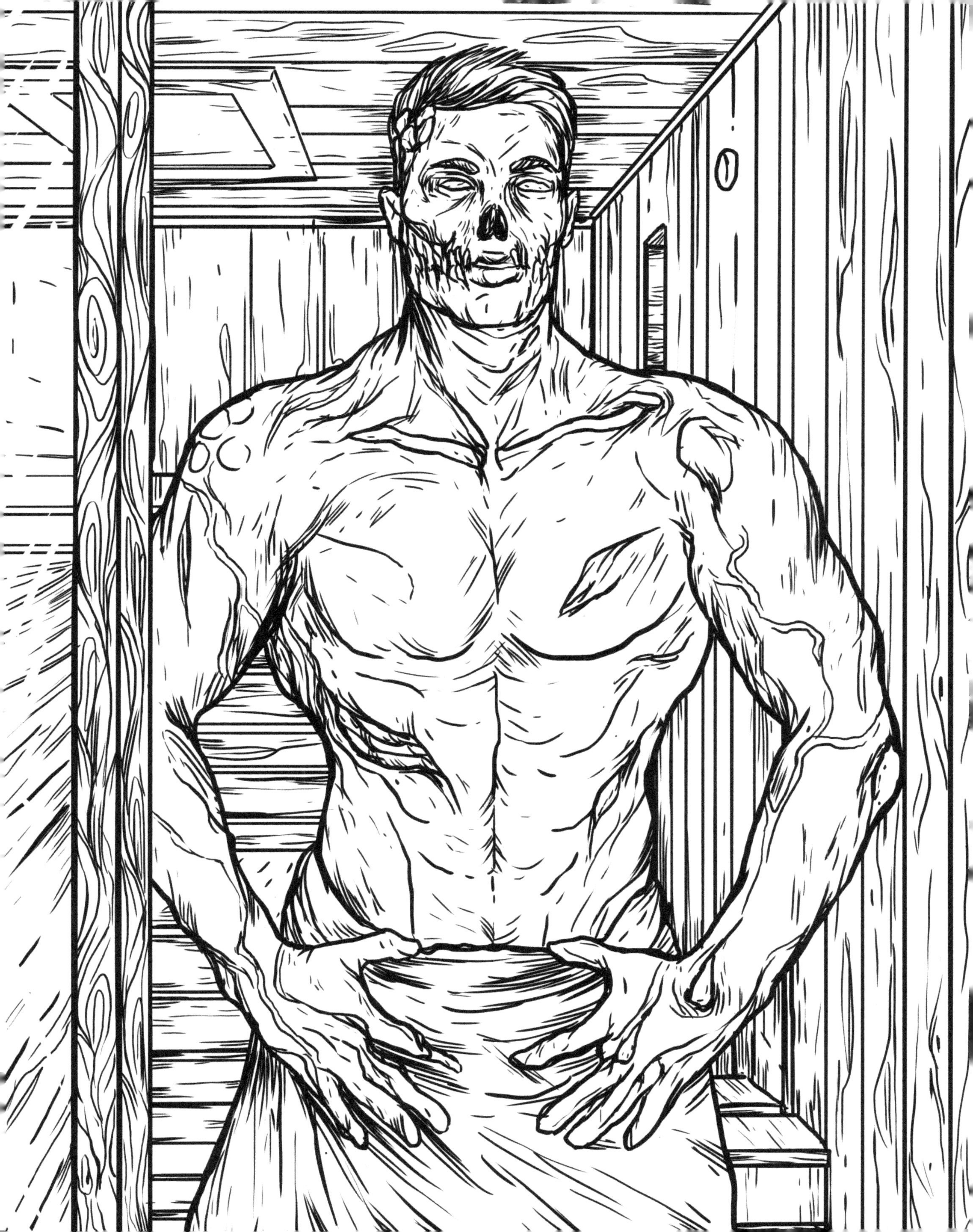

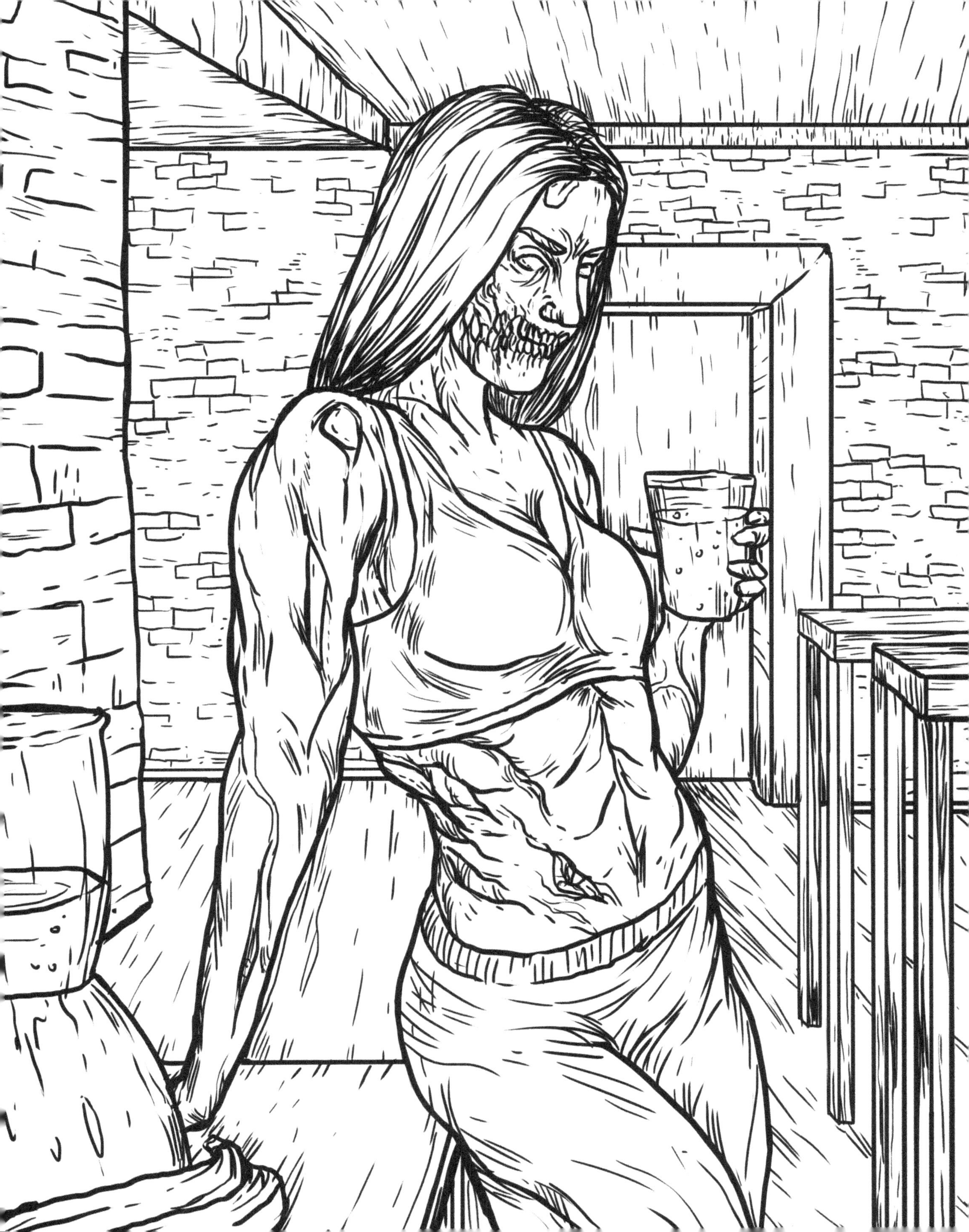

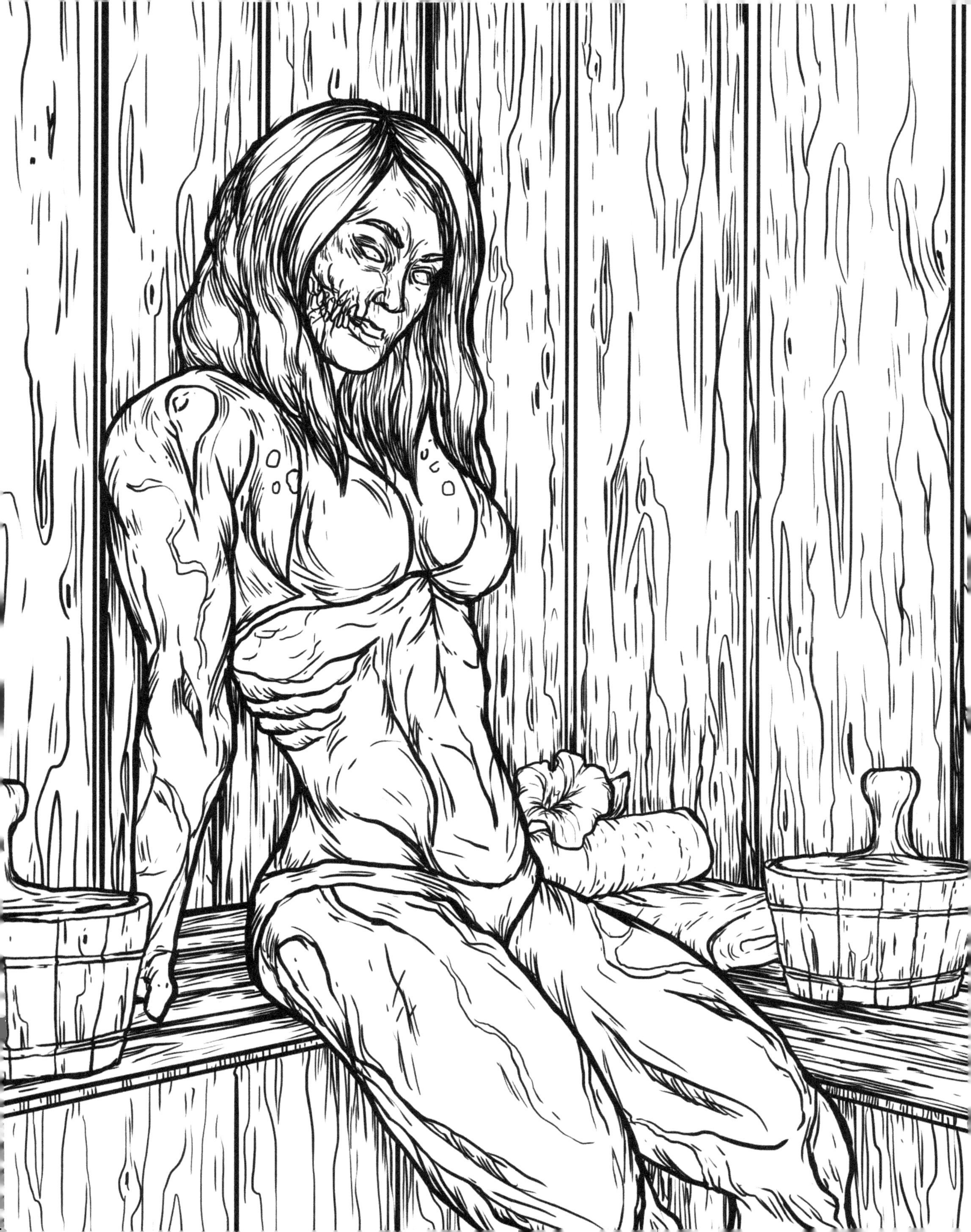